WILDER AND SUNNY

The Adventures of
Wilder Good

THE ADVENTURES OF

#**3**

The Adventures of
Wilder Good

WILDER AND SUNNY

S. J. DAHLSTROM

Illustrations by Cliff Wilke

PAUL DRY BOOKS
Philadelphia   2015

First Paul Dry Books Edition, 2015

Paul Dry Books, Inc.
Philadelphia, Pennsylvania
www.pauldrybooks.com

Printed in the United States of America

CIP data available at the Library of Congress
ISBN-13: 978-1-58988-100-6

for Harry Jack—
may you find a woman with a heart
like your Mother's.

CONTENTS

After all these years, I see that I was mistaken about Eve in the beginning; it is better to live outside the Garden with her, than inside it without her.

MARK TWAIN
Adam's Diary

WILDER AND SUNNY

CHAPTER ONE

Sunny

The first time Wilder Good saw Sunny Parker was also the first time, and one of the few times, he had touched her. Or rather she had touched him, meaning her cowboy boot had left a long red mark down the side of his head.

That was back in the second grade a few weeks after Christmas when he had moved to Cottonwood, Colorado. On Wilder's first day at the new school, he wandered friendless around the cold playground with his jacket buttoned up to his neck. He absent-mindedly walked under the monkey bars, and with a great surprising crash, Sunny landed right on top of him. She was full of laughter—that's what he remembered most—even though her boot heel had struck his head, ear, and cheek as she fell, leaving a significant scratch. It had been an accident, Wilder's fault even, but she had apologized, sincere and sweet as she had been taught. Then she turned and ran off with her friends, blond hair blowing in the frigid Colorado wind.

That was how they had met, in the second grade when girls are only friends with girls and boys are only friends with boys. But that wasn't quite true for Sunny and Wilder.

For since that day, to Wilder, there had been no other girl in the world like Sunny. She wasn't a tomboy, she wasn't girly, she was just . . . unbridled. She was the freest person he had ever known. And now, at 12 years old, even though Wilder's sampling size of females was pretty small, she was a completely different species. He seemed to have recognized this from the start. They never referred to each other as boyfriend and girlfriend, as their parents never allowed childish romantic attachments to foster, but they had a unique, if unspoken, bond.

And so, to see her tear up and to hear her whimpered cry unlocked a piece of him he didn't know very well yet, but that feeling was as real as the lime green walls of the junior high school lunchroom they were standing in. It pierced him.

As innocent as a fawn, Boone had walked up to Sunny while she talked with her friends after lunch. With a faked, enamored shyness he asked, "Hey Sunny, can I see your smile?"

Wilder was watching from behind. Even if he sometimes completely ignored her when she was around, he always kind of kept an eye on her.

Sunny smiled her big beautiful smile not as an answer to an order, just an unguarded reaction to Boone's request. Her lips spread across her teeth revealing the crooked 'V' her front teeth made. Her two front teeth hadn't come in right, and she had told Wilder in private that her parents were making her wait a few more years for braces. But still, she was a girl becoming a woman, and she was aware of the imperfect line of her top teeth when she looked in a mirror. It had not stopped her from smiling, however.

Boone pointed at the crooked teeth and started laughing and looking around to get everyone's attention. Kids looked at Sunny and laughed.

"BENT TEETH!" he said.

Sunny had a lot of steel in her entrenched behind her hazel eyes—you could see that from ten feet away. But she was also a young girl with a sincere and transparent tenderness. She had her weak spots, and Boone knew just how to reach this one. Her eyes filled with tears, and when she wiped them quickly in a show of bravery, they filled again.

Wilder heard the remark and walked up to Sunny, past Boone, and stood in front of her, shielding her. He didn't put his arm around her, he just put himself between her and the bully. Wilder's heart beat fast, and he felt a drumming in his ears. He felt hot, but not sweaty. He felt red. He didn't know what to say. The friends Sunny had been talking with laughed too but were now trying to hide their smirks by clasping their hands over their mouths. Wilder was overcome. He was not in a rage, exactly, but his heart had taken over his body. It made his head swim a little bit.

Wilder turned and squared up to Boone, who was in the eighth grade. He knew he had to say something. Somewhere in the back of his mind, Wilder also knew he would have to take swats if there was a fight. But it wasn't a debate for him; he was going to defend Sunny. Boone was bigger than everyone else, and he knew it. He had bullied Wilder—and everyone else—for years, but Wilder had always been able to blow it off. He had been raised to turn the other cheek. But humiliating Sunny felt different, drastically different.

Boone was big, but he was also soft and he had never had anyone, especially not an underclassman seventh-grader, stand up to him. He had at least a three-inch height advantage and outweighed the skinny Wilder by 40 pounds.

"Boone, apologize to Sunny for saying that." Wilder said, his voice fluttering a bit with this untested courage. He knew he was crossing a line that couldn't be crossed back over. If he threw a punch, he wanted it to be a good one, and he wanted Boone to see it coming. He heard his dad's voice in his head, "Go for the nose."

"Or what?" Boone answered, as all bullies do. He puffed out his chest and took a step toward Wilder and pushed him with both hands. Wilder was braced, and while he was skinny, he was wiry, so the push didn't have the intent Boone expected. Boone's eyes widened a bit when Wilder didn't step back with his shove.

Wilder tightened his right fist into a mesquite knot and swung for the nose. He didn't know what else to do. He had never punched anyone before, not seriously, and surely not in the face, but he swung as hard as he could like he had been told and had read about in so many Louis L'Amour books. He drove his fist forward from deep in his cowboy boots, from his waist and from his arm . . . and he followed through like he was throwing a baseball.

The punch made a skin on skin sound, like

the sharp *crack* of a small green pine branch breaking in an ice storm.

The big boy went down like he was on roller skates. He grabbed his nose, and blood poured down and was soon in his mouth and lips and down the front of his shirt.

He was stunned and speechless lying there on the cafeteria's cold floor. For his part, Wilder just stood there, braced low like in the triple-threat position he had learned at basketball practice; his hands were up and clenched. And he had no idea what to do next.

Everything went quiet. Then, behind him, he heard Sunny run out of the lunch room crying.

CHAPTER TWO

Decisions and Consequences

That was pretty much the end of it. Several teachers who saw the interaction and the ensuing punch had dispersed the crowd and walked the boys out of the cafeteria in separate directions.

The two boys were now reunited, sitting in separate chairs in the principal's office in front of the big desk of big Mr. Breaux (which was pronounced "bro"). Boone had gotten cleaned up and was now wearing his sweat-stained mesh basketball practice jersey. He held a handful of bloody napkins in his lap and kept sniffing up the blood in his nose.

Mrs. Brann, who was also Wilder's English teacher, had seen the punch, and sat between the two boys with her back straight in her wool skirt and blouse. She was in her late 60s and loved Wilder and encouraged his poetry. The three of them sat in silence waiting for Mr. Breaux to come in. The fluorescent lights hummed above them.

Wilder thought about many things and felt ashamed of being in the principal's office, but he couldn't help thinking of his planned weekend fishing trip with his old man mentor, Gale Loving—a trip that was now certainly to be canceled by his parents. They were going to fly-fish on the Rio Grande river on Saturday. He was angry at himself and knew Gale would be disappointed too. His gear was already packed in his room. It was the last week of school and all the June insect hatches were about to make the trout feeding frenzy come alive.

When Mr. Breaux finally came in he went over to the paddle hanging on the wall by a leather wrist loop. Mr. Breaux was 6'4" and about 300 pounds, so he was wide and thick. His fingers looked like sausages. He picked up the paddle and gently laid it across the front of the desk for the boys to see. It had white canvas athletic tape wrapped around the handle to make for a good grip, which had turned brown on the edges and then black in the center from repeated use. The paddle's fat center sweet spot was two feet long and six inches wide.

Wilder didn't gulp exactly, but his eyes got big and his heart beat fast. He was at full attention. Boone wept.

Wilder had gotten numerous licks at home as he grew up, as well as at school, though never from Breaux, and he was under no illusions about what was coming. He didn't expect mercy and knew that licks at school meant licks at home too. But that didn't mean he enjoyed it. He was big enough to get significant swats, and they hurt.

Mr. Breaux thumbed and read in silence through the two files on his desk and the incident report written in perfect flowing script by Mrs. Brann. Then he looked up at the boys.

"You boys were fighting, I see?" lifting his eyebrows up from the paperwork.

They both nodded, and Mr. Breaux proceeded to let each boy tell his story, then Mrs. Brann. They each got the story mainly right except for Boone's part where he was adamant that it was all just a joke, which in his mind should have acquitted him of any wrong doing. Mr. Breaux didn't respond to his argument. Then he spoke,

"Boys, I like to joke. And I like to laugh. I really do. I even like to laugh at people. People are funny." He leaned back and patted his round belly and smiled and said, "We all need to learn to not take ourselves too seriously."

He paused for ten long seconds as he looked around the room letting the boys stew. After 30 years, he was an expert at teaching lessons.

He liked his job and he liked kids, especially this kind of interaction.

"But," he began again, "there are two ways to laugh at other people. One is to laugh at the things they can change—like an ugly shirt or a bad hair day or tripping in the hall. That's funny, laugh it up. But the other is laughing about things a person *can't* change. When you pick on someone about those things—like family stuff or body stuff . . . or teeth. Well, you are crossing a line. That is when you hurt people. You can hurt their hearts, and it's not funny."

Mr. Breaux focused on Boone and looked him deep in the eye. "Do you understand what I am saying?"

Boone nodded. Mr. Breaux paused again. Fifteen seconds ticked by.

"So," he continued, "let's wrap this little deal up. All our decisions in life have consequences—good and bad. Fighting gets two days in-school suspension or two licks. Boone, your parents have signed our form saying no swats, so your ISS will begin today. Wilder, we both know what your folks say. What'll it be?"

"I'll take the swats." Wilder gulped and swallowed hard and dry.

"OK. Boone you may leave and report to ISS. Mrs. Brann, will you stay and be my witness?"

Boone left looking sober but relieved. Mrs. Brann stood up and straightened her skirt. She seemed to be fighting tears, but she stiffened—and then sniffled a bit, Wilder thought, when Breaux gave him the direction, "Grip the chair and look forward."

Wilder stood up and did as he was told and his heart raced like he was about to be shot by a firing squad. No matter how many swats Wilder got, it was always fresh, every time. He set his mind not to cry, although he felt sort of mushy inside. His jaw and his eyes set hard, following his mind, and he braced for the blows.

Breaux made quick work and delivered the swats with conviction. Two loud pops, about four seconds apart. Then Wilder stood up. His rear was on fire. He fought tears of pain, and guilt, but one bulging drop snuck out and tumbled down his cheek. He caught it and wiped it off quickly. Wilder's heart was tender. He now only thought of his mother and how this would upset her.

"Mrs. Brann, thank you. You can go. Wilder, you may go to the bathroom and wash your face and walk it off. Please come back in here when you are done."

Wilder did so and returned in three minutes, determined to put on a good face. He knew he had been wrong to punch Boone, and he had been taught to take his medicine. He wasn't mad at Mr. Breaux. He sat down again in the office on his still red-hot bottom. It was in the throbbing stage, already past the initial searing burn.

"Wilder, I want to talk to you man to man. When men talk it stays just between them. It's not a secret, but it is a sign of respect, between two men. Understand?"

"Yes, sir."

"Wilder, you probably did a great favor for Boone today. You made him a better boy. There is generally only one cure for bullies, and he got his dose. He is not a bad kid, but I think he needed that like a boil needs to be lanced. And you stood up for a smaller kid who was being bullied. That is honorable. I am proud of you. You will be a fine man someday, I have no doubt."

Wilder wept. He didn't know why. It just kind of broke loose. The words of affirmation and grace made him sob for several moments as his thin chest heaved in and out. Mr. Breaux paused again and let him get it out.

"But, I have something else to tell you too. You cannot solve the world's problems with your fists . . . or bombs or guns or whatever it may be. The only person in the world you can control is you. If you start down a line of fighting everybody who says what you don't like, or does what you don't like, you will have a hard life. I don't think that is your future, son, but I want you to know that there are better methods for beating bullies than with your fists."

Wilder nodded.

Mr. Breaux stood up and motioned for Wilder to do the same. The big man beamed an equally big smile down at the boy and said, "Before you go back to class, do you want to sign the paddle?"

The back side of the paddle was covered in names. Wilder smiled and took the paddle and the pen that Breaux handed him and found a spot just above where his best friend, Gary Beggs, had signed his nickname, "BIG," in all caps. It had six little marks next to it, and Wilder smirked thinking about Big getting into trouble all the time.

Wilder just wrote his brand, the running WG. Mr. Breaux gave him a solid pat on the back, which counted as a hug.

ᴜᴄ

CHAPTER THREE
'When do I fight?'

Wilder dragged his feet coming into the house that afternoon as he unloaded off the school bus with Molly. Her eyes had grown big when she saw him, and she looked at him like he was some sort of three-headed alien.

She whispered to him in a frightened bewilderment, "You really hit someone?"

Wilder told her to hush. Molly stiffened and said, "You're rude."

Molly had heard about the fight through the grapevine that ran all the way down to her fourth grade class. The standard rule in their house was that any punishment received at school was doubled at home. So Wilder feared a few more swats from his dad, and also that his fishing trip would be canceled.

Wilder's mom, Livy, was in the kitchen when the children entered the double-wide trailer house. Wilder wanted to get it over with, the sooner the better, so he threw his school backpack on the couch and headed into the kitchen. Livy was peeling potatoes, and he saw two packages of cube steak thawing on the counter. Cube steak meant only one thing in their house: chicken fried steak, which was Wilder's favorite food.

Livy looked over at him and dried her hands on her apron and walked towards her son. She bent down and gave him a warm hug. Wilder tensed up, surprised, not sure what the affection was for. Livy broke the hug after several seconds and looked at him straight, holding him away from her with a hand on each of his shoulders. She looked long into his eyes, searching them, and gripped his growing muscles with her thin hands.

"Yes," she said, "you are good, Wilder Whitaker Good."

Wilder returned her gaze with a puzzled expression.

"I just wanted to check and make sure again. I know you had a rough day, but you are good . . . and strong, and I am proud of you. You are beautiful, inside and out, and I love you."

"Mom, you know what happened at school today, right?"

"Yes," Livy let him go and looked out the window, picking up a half-peeled potato and resuming her work, "I know all about it. You showed chivalry, and you accepted the consequences like a man. I wouldn't have my son do any different. Mr. Breaux and your father can direct you in the best methods for this kind of situation, that is theirs to teach. But as your mother, I am proud of you." She turned and looked at him again.

"You have always had my heart, son, but you keep finding ways to win it a little more every day."

Livy sniffled, and Wilder stood there stunned. She quickly wiped her nose with her wrist, still holding a potato.

"Now go and do your chores and your homework, and I'm sure your dad will have some thoughts for you when he gets home."

Wilder nodded and felt his heart hope a little. The gloom that had come over him lifted a bit. His mother could always do that for him. She was the only person he knew who ever said the word "beautiful." It made him use the word too, and to watch for beauty, in his own way.

Wilder changed clothes and put on jeans with holes in the knees and his work boots. He fed and watered the chickens in the back yard, leaving the 11 eggs he counted for Molly to collect. He refilled his dog's water bowl, freshening the stale hot water. Huck trotted over and lapped it up like he had been dying of thirst in the Sahara desert all day. Huck was named after *Huckleberry Finn*, a book Wilder had read several times. Wilder wrestled the big yellow lab for about ten minutes until he was breathless. Wilder only weighed 125 pounds, and Huck about 80, so it was of course a bloodless, but pretty fair fight. Huck was in his prime and loved to play and wrestle as all labs do, but he never used his teeth or claws when he tussled with Wilder.

Wilder took out the trash from every place in the house, which wasn't necessary but he thought it wouldn't hurt to muster all the good will he could. When he got out the lawnmower to cut the grass, which he had cut only four days ago, Livy hollered from the kitchen window and told him to stop and do his homework. He did so, all the time ignoring his fly-fishing gear neatly arranged in his room. He was itching to get a few casts in for practice, but knew he had better leave it be and not get his hopes up.

Wilder's dad, Hank, came in an hour later, covered in a thin coat of sweat and sawdust that had stuck to his face and arms and clothes. Every father has a smell, and Hank smelled like fine pine sawdust. Wilder thought it was a good way for a dad to smell. He could tell what type of work his dad had been doing each day by the shape and smell of the sawdust. Larger chunky pieces meant framing; fine white dust, finish work; red sawdust, cedar decking; mud on his boots, site preparation.

Wilder was in the backyard by then, under the big cottonwood tree carving a slingshot. He had already carved about a hundred slingshots, but he could never pass up a perfect fork on a branch when he saw one. He would cut and carve them expertly—and then leave them lying around in the backyard. Only rarely did he finish one with rubber straps and a leather patch for the shot.

Hank walked out the back door and stood on the deck, which he and Wilder had built last summer. It was a stunning yellow pine deck that stood in stark contrast to the old trailer house it backed up to. Wilder saw his dad and walked over to him with his head down. He didn't know what to say, so he just stood there.

Hank moved down the wide wood steps of the deck and caught Wilder's eye and motioned for him to sit down next to him. He did, and father and son sat side by side looking out into the woods behind their home.

"I'm not going to bust you, since I know you're wondering about that," Hank began.

Wilder nodded and fought the urge to ask about the fishing trip.

"A father never wants his son to get into trouble, but sometimes trouble finds you. That's the hard part. But it is still up to us to choose how and when we will fight back. There is a pull toward violence in men that can destroy you."

Wilder didn't completely understand, but he nodded. His dad didn't talk very much, so when he did Wilder knew it was important.

"But when *do* I fight, Dad?" Wilder asked.

"Every man has to answer that question for himself. There is no simple answer. I'm not saying that you made the right or wrong choice in punching that boy today. There is a time for war and a time for peace. There are so many good things to this world, son, but it can be vicious too. But you need to look for other options before fighting—that's what I want you to hear from me. A man who rushes to a fight is a fool. Here's the question you need to ask yourself, 'Did I do everything possible to prevent this?

"But then, the few times in life you have to fight something and commit to action, hit first and hit hard, like you did today. Don't be double-minded about it."

"Well, Dad," Wilder replied in earnest, "I went for the nose like you said."

Hank smiled and patted his son on the back, muffling a chuckle. "Yes, I guess you did.

"But I never want to hear any gossip or bragging or bullying after this. What's done is done. Show that boy grace and humility, and try to make him your friend, if you can."

"Yes, sir"

Hank stood up, and Wilder knew that was the end of it. The boy walked down the steps and back into the yard.

"And Wilder," Hank called back toward the yard, "I am proud that my son would stand up for his friend." He smiled knowingly as he added, "Sunny is worth it."

Wilder turned and smiled under his gray felt cowboy hat, and somehow he knew the fishing trip was still on.

CHAPTER FOUR

Off Wildering

Two days later Wilder was waiting by the window in the living room at seven AM when he heard the "slap, slap, slap" of Gale's diesel pickup as it pulled into the driveway. He couldn't see inside the truck for the dawn light just coming up and windows being tinted, but he knew the sound of that truck like a school bell. Wilder grabbed his rod—it was a three-piece broken down in a black case—and his backpack, which was a recent upgrade. It had been sent to him by his Grampa Whit who lived on Long Island in New York. It was a leather-trimmed, tan canvas Filson. With rod case in hand he rushed out of the house leaving the screen door to smack in the morning stillness. The new backpack bounced on his shoulders as he ran. It was stuffed with his usual day-trip survival gear including a water bottle.

The air was foggy on the perfect June morning, and in that misty light Wilder couldn't have been more shocked or confused when he opened the front passenger door of the truck and saw someone sitting in his usual seat.

"SURPRISE!" Sunny yelled at him face to face from about a foot away. Her crooked front teeth were framed by a huge smile that began to crack and turn into bright laughs. She sat there buckled into the big front seat, with blue jeans on and two long blond braids running down her shoulders, bouncing on a pearl-snap shirt as she laughed. Gale laughed too, and they both stared down at Wilder who stood frozen in a leaning-into-the-pickup stance.

"Get in, pup," Gale broke the shock of the moment. "We're losing time to get on the river."

"Yeah, Wilder, get in," Sunny said as she unbuckled, "You sit up front with your 'old man' . . . as you call him." She laughed again.

"Ummm, no, that's fine. You can sit there."

"We can all fit up front. You can just scoot over and ride in the middle, Sunny" Gale offered.

"No, I'll be fine in the back," Wilder insisted, if put off a bit at the surprise. "Gale, I was hoping I could bring Huck today. Is that all right? He'll stay close to us. He's a good dog."

"Sure. Get him and let's go."

Still unsettled by the sudden appearance of Sunny, Wilder threw his gear in the back seat and ran around the side of the house to get Huck, who seemed to know he had been invited—he was at the back gate bouncing up and down like a pogo stick, his head and long lab ears just peeking over the top of the gate for half a second with every jump.

As Wilder unlatched the gate the big dog flew through the opening, knocking him over. But Huck was soon back in "heel" position as the boy hollered and instructed the eager dog. Wilder and Huck loaded into the backseat, and Gale turned west toward the river they would be fishing today, the Rio Grande.

As the truck sped up, Sunny, bursting at the seams like always, turned in her seat to Wilder in the back.

"I get to go off wildering with you two. Pretty surprised, huh? We were all in on it. Gale, your mom and dad, and my folks too. Haha." She laughed and laughed.

"What's wildering?" Wilder mumbled, but he knew what she meant.

"Oh, just what you always do. Wildering off in the wilderness."

Wilder sat and listened as Sunny explained the whole deal. After the fight, Wilder's dad had called her dad, Jack Parker, just to make sure the story on Sunny's end matched up with the story from school and to see if Wilder needed to apologize for anything. The story had been the same of course, and Jack had been so thankful and impressed with Wilder that as the men talked, and the fishing trip was mentioned, both fathers thought that letting the kids spend a day fishing together would be a good way to release whatever tension might still exist. Jack Parker managed and lived on a big ranch with his family. He had a pretty simple definition of a man. Wilder had met it, evidently.

As Wilder listened he understood that it was a special reward of sorts that was being given to him, but he couldn't help feeling as if his little domain with Gale had been invaded. And even though it was invaded by Sunny, his secret girlfriend (in his mind only), and the one person in the world whom he actually looked forward to seeing every day at school, he just didn't know how to act. When he was alone with Gale, Wilder was completely at ease. Now his stomach was tied up in those knots that this beautiful girl always prompted.

Wilder fell back on his manners in an attempt to cover his disappointment.

"Well, that's good, Sunny. But Gale and I aren't just playing fishermen today." Wilder said, falsely including Gale in his childish aloofness. "We plan on fishing big water. I hope you can keep up."

"Oh, yeah, I'll keep up. I brought my fishing pole and worms." Sunny was immune to subtle insults. She was still too pure in spirit to understand or interpret them. Wilder rolled his eyes at this response. Fly-fisherman use "rods" not "poles." Wilder had been careful to make his fly-fishing education as pretentious as possible, but this time he kept it to himself.

And so they drove and talked and ate the hot sandwiches that Gale's wife, Lucille, had packed for them—eggs and bacon and cheese on heavily buttered toast. She had even sent a small bottle of Tabasco for Wilder since she knew he liked it. Gale sipped coffee for most of the hour it took to drive to the river access point. Huck watched intently as the fragrant sandwiches disappeared, which Wilder noticed and handed his dog the crusts from his last corner, but they didn't have any bacon between them. Then Huck sat and drummed his tail on the seat next to Wilder, "whap, whap, whap," all the way there.

Somehow the dog knew they were getting close, and he stood up on the seat and began to whine as Gale slowed down on the two-lane highway.

ᗯᕲ

CHAPTER FIVE

Big Waters

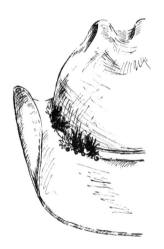

Gale pulled off the highway and onto a gravel road in the now bright morning sunlight. They parked at the trailhead for Gallinas Canyon, a quarter mile from the highway, with the big Rio Grande roaring by just a little ways off the parking area. The Rio Grande runs all the way down to the Gulf of Mexico, winding through the dry country of the Texas/Mexico border, but its headwaters on the Upper Rio flow through mountains. The water is clear and cold and fast, particularly in the spring. The canyon had strewn the river with boulders, and the large rocks littered the river as the wild water crashed and flowed downhill from spring snow melt. It was big water.

The three fishermen spilled out of the truck and started rigging up their rods near the back of the pickup. Huck had jumped to the ground when the door opened and disappeared on the bank of the river. Sunny was ready to go immediately. All she had was a bare hook on her spin-cast rod and worms to thread onto it. She smiled broadly as she watched the boys go about their ruminations, piecing together their rods and threading their lines and choosing and tying on flies. Mainly she was thinking and planning for lunch.

"What did you bring for lunch in your little bag, Wilder?"

"Nothing. And that's not a little bag. It's called a rucksack."

"A rucksack? What's a rucksack? It looks like a bag to me."

"Well it's not."

"Then what is it?"

"A rucksack."

"What is ruck?"

"Guy stuff. You wouldn't understand."

"OK then, does your rucksack have any lunch in it?"

"No."

"What are you going to eat for lunch?"

"Fish." Wilder mumbled as he was tying on his favorite fly—the pheasant-tail bead head #12—to his tippet. He didn't look up from the improved clinch knot, which he had just put in his mouth to moisten it before he pulled it tight. The spit ensured that the knot would slip and tighten with no slack. Wilder then cut off the end close to the fly with small nippers that hung around his neck by a leather string.

"Oh yeah," Sunny laughed, "that's a great idea. I didn't think of that. We'll just eat fish."

Wilder rolled his eyes where Sunny could see it this time.

"Of course I'm going to eat fish. We *are* going fishing."

"What if you don't catch any?"

"Yeah, right." Wilder was beginning to enjoy himself now; his bragging could get into gear. "I can probably catch every fish in this river by noon."

Sunny smiled and nodded, but not in mocking.

"Oh I hope so. I love trout." Sunny's eyes twinkled. "What fly are you using first?"

"Pheasant-tail bead head."

"Why?"

"It looks good to eat."

That cracked Sunny up. "Wilder, you're ridiculous."

Wilder smiled too. "Well, it does. I would eat it if I was a fish. It has a head like insects do. I like insects with heads. Shiny heads."

"Well you're not a fish, but I hope they agree with you."

"I think like a fish."

"How does a fish think?"

"Sunny, I can't teach you everything in one day . . ." Wilder mumbled and feigned annoyance.

Gale smiled at the kids' bantering as he put on his waders and leaned back against the lowered tailgate of the truck to rig his rod and first choice of fly. They would be fishing nymphs today, which were called "wet flies." Wet flies would drift down the river under the surface of the water, swimming like aquatic insects in the nymph stage of development. Dry flies were generally much smaller and made to resemble winged insects that floated or fell onto the water's surface. Dry-fly fishing was good for evening hatches on still, slow moving water.

There were lots of nymphs to choose from, but Wilder wasn't going to ask Gale which one he was going to use. Gale wouldn't offer advice unless asked. He had been fly-fishing for most of his 72 years and had guided in little mountain towns up and down the Rockies in his twenties. During the winter months he tied his own flies.

Wilder didn't have waders, and his rod was an older, eight-foot nine-weight rod that Gale had given him. On most of his adventures with Gale, Wilder didn't have his own gear, but he didn't mind too much. He was planning his own collection all along and doing the research on what to get when he had the money.

What he did have was his own aluminum fly box with a great collection of flies, some he tied himself. He had spent hours over the winter at Gale's house, in his shop, inventing and constructing crazy looking flies with all the fly-tying materials Gale had collected. His flies were made of all sorts of natural material like bird feathers and rabbit fur and deer hair. They weren't usually "correct" or very complex, but he had caught fish on a few of them. Catching a fish with your own hand-tied fly meant you were part of a special little club for fly-fishermen. And thanks to Gale, at only 12 years old, Wilder was in that club.

Wilder had tied one fly that he called the A-bomb. It had actually caught a fish once, or so Wilder said. It was a huge size #2/0 hook, which had a real mouse tail tied to the end. It had hopper legs and caddis fly wings made from Mallard wing feathers, and a long, 360-degree hackle made from Huck's yellow lab shoulder fur. This was all set behind a massive golden bead head. Wilder called it a "bomb" because it made a "plop" when it hit the water.

Wilder treasured his collection of flies and hated when he lost one in the river, which rarely happened because he was willing to do just about anything to retrieve a hung fly off the river bottom or a fallen tree. He would never just jerk his line until it broke. If a fly was hung up, he was going in after it.

But Wilder's best flies, the ones in his Hall of Fame as he called it, were stuck into the band of his ever-present gray felt cowboy hat. Each one of these flies had been in a fish's mouth; some had caught multiple fish. When a fly had done its job in this way, Wilder usually retired it to the hat. There were twenty or so flies up there now, beginning with a string of four pheasant-tail bead heads.

Wilder glanced over and saw that Gale was tying on a large hairy looking fly. He didn't recognize it. Sunny was kneeling on the ground, pinching a large night crawler in half and threading her hook through the slimy, dirty, twisting half worm. She wiped her hand on her blue jeans, and Wilder remembered that this was quite a girl, both tender and tough. He was glad she was here, he thought, and then he had a wave of that strange girl feeling roll over him. She was that word his mom used, "beautiful." She was butterfly beautiful.

Rigged up and ready, they turned to the grassy footpath that led to the river's edge.

Huck had joined them. The big, and now soaking, Labrador was at Wilder's left side. At the bank they stopped and let the river and the canyon pour into them. The wind in the 50-foot pine and fir and spruce trees swished through the millions of evergreen needles and made the quaking aspens move just enough so that they tinkled back and forth like little bells. The water roared with a deep consistent hum as it was ferociously dragged downhill by gravity, and in all of this sound there was nothing unpleasant. It was noisy enough to make you talk a bit louder to be heard over the native symphony, but even that was pleasant. They talked louder, but it also seemed a reverential whisper, a hushed yell. And with the canyon now washed in a heavy light-yellow from the morning sun, Wilder thought that Eden must have been close to Colorado.

Gale turned to the kids to say something, but as he opened his mouth Wilder pointed across the river and made a polite "Shhhh" movement with his hand.

They crouched down in unison to see a large dark animal coming down the steep mountainside that fell into the river on the opposite bank. It was a cow elk picking her way through the rocks and downed timber and brush. She was almost directly across the river from them which was about 65 feet wide at this point. She looked sick and strange, being off by herself was one thing, but she also was thin and her coat was thick and rough looking, as opposed to the thinning and slick-looking summer coat most elk were developing by now.

The three of them moved in a silent hunter's crouch to a boulder a few yards away and rested against it. They peeked up over the top to watch the elk. She was going to cross the river and come out, presumably, right next to them. Everyone's eyes were fixed and wide open to watch the elk at close range.

She reached the bottom and took a step into the river, finding her footing in the swirling cold water. Rocks were everywhere under the surface and sticking out above the water. The elk caught herself from a slight stumble and moved out into the water with all four feet.

About midstream the water came up to her chest, about three and a half feet deep, and as she stepped in front of a large car-sized boulder with water roaring past each side of it, she slipped into the cloudy water to mid-chest and held there for a second . . . and then the entire elk disappeared beneath the water's surface.

She didn't bounce back up. Wilder and Sunny gaped. Gale's mouth tightened.

They watched for several minutes in silence,

scanning the water downstream and then back to the spot where she had vanished. No sign of the elk.

"Gale, what happened?" Sunny finally turned and asked. She looked shaken, like a little of the wind had been knocked out of her.

"The current took her. She wasn't strong enough to get back up," Gale replied.

They all stood up straight now. They understood—the elk was dead, drowned and wedged somewhere under the boulder.

"Wow, I just can't believe it." Wilder said in awe. "I've never seen anything like that."

"She looked sick and on her way out anyway. I've seen a lot of elk make it through one last winter and then give out in spring. But then," Gale turned his gaze from the river to the kids, "every elk dies.

"A lot of animals and people go into the mountains and never come out. Remember that. They give and take away. These big rivers are plenty of fun and good for a day of fishing. But never forget that they can kill you too. That was a 700-pound animal, dead now under only four feet of water. If the river gets the first punch, it'll probably win."

Gale caught Wilder's eyes, and he knew Gale was acknowledging the school fight. Then Gale looked back and forth from Wilder to Sunny with a serious eye, making sure he had their attention.

"I want you to explore the river and have fun today, but let's stay where we can see each other. And you two, stay close together."

Wilder and Sunny both said "Yes, sir," and they meant it.

〜

CHAPTER SIX
Fly-fishing

It was nine-thirty now. The cool mountain night of 36 degrees had quickly baked away and it was in the 50s, although it was easy to feel hot as the close mountain sun warmed the thin air of the canyon and the light reflected up from the big water. Gale marched upstream along the bank to give the kids some distance. He wanted to catch some fish, and to do that he would need to get away from kids and dog and all the playing he knew would ensue between Wilder and Sunny. Gale no longer kept any fish, for the most part. He was almost exclusively a catch and release fisherman now. But he still loved the feel of a trout on his line.

The old man had been a fly-fisherman before it was trendy, which meant before there were movies about it and thousands of contraptions marketers had invented to drape all over his body for a day's fishing. He carried no landing net and wore no fly vest. Every piece of gear that he used was time-tested and modified in little ways that suited only him.

He wore a felt cowboy hat when he fished; it had no particular shape to it from years of mountain showers that made the brim droop down all the way around. He had no cowboy vanity, like Wilder, which demanded he keep the brim shaped with exactly the right crease all the time. That was something the boy had inherited from his Papa Milam.

Besides his rod, Gale packed only a fly box in his pocket, a small spool of tippet, an extra leader, and a set of clamp pliers with gold finger loops, which were always closed on the flap of his shirt pocket. He used this tool to cut line, smash split shot on to his tippet, and unhook the fish he caught. He wore wool shirts almost exclusively, of different thicknesses, and all the lighter summer ones had worn places on the pockets where the fishing clamp dangled during the spring and summer fishing season.

His one upgrade over the years was to use graphite rods. Having been raised on split bamboo since he began fishing—which was all that was available to him—he had always hated the fiberglass rods that began to appear 40 years ago. They separated him from the fish, he couldn't feel them at all. But the new graphite rods were better, and he had adopted them. Perhaps also, because his split bamboo rods were special to him now, and he didn't want to risk breaking them. The rods hung on the wall of his shop at home and seemed to him like old friends. He took them down from time to time to dust them and feel their superb natural action. Wilder did this too.

Gale had tied on a woolly booger #4, black. It had a large golden bead on the front to catch and reflect sunlight as the nymph drifted along the river bottom. He knew the stoneflies were moving and hatching now, and his big dark fly was perfect for the cloudy water. Trout needed to see the insects moving in the water from a close distance. The woolly booger seemed to imitate the year round food source of a swimming leech as well. Whatever it actually resembled, fish liked it and it was a good fly for in between distinct hatches. It was still a bit early to fish a straight stonefly nymph, and the woolly booger would pull in lots of trout still looking for numerous other insects—at least that's the way he figured it. It was too early for mayfly and caddis as well.

Gale clamped two small split shot onto his tippet with his fishing clamp and continued to move upriver until he was about 50 yards away from the kids. Then he stopped and stared and read the water like a book. He didn't just start casting. He noted the pockets and the riffles and the feeding areas and the resting areas. Trout stay near the riffles where the fresh oxygenated water sparkles down to them and then rises back up like champagne in a glass. They sit and watch and breathe and eventually their food comes down these little creases in the water.

Gale was happy with any fish, but he primarily worked the water where only a big fish might live. He wanted to catch old fish, like himself, ones that seemed to have a little gray hair, like himself. He wanted to outsmart them.

Squinting his eyes at the morning sun's reflection on the water, shining like a million diamonds floating on the surface, he found his pool and stretched his rod out with his right arm and with two beats back and forth shot his fly line out like a long arcing arrow and let his nymph swim the current. He stood in about 20 inches of water and the familiar feeling of the cold water pressing against his legs felt good. It felt strong.

He had been right about the hole, but wrong about the kind of fish it held. He felt a little tug and didn't set the hook but let the small fish take it, although he didn't see it. He knew it was small by what the rod told him and through his finger holding the line under the shaft, just off the reel. He never played the little ones. He liked to catch them, but he knew they had less energy and wanted to get them free of the hook as soon as possible. He reeled fast, knowing his rod and 4x tippet could handle the pressure. The silvery and red-streaked trout popped out of the water like a little rocket, and Gale tugged and skipped it across the top of the stream, gently but quickly. He saw that it was a cutthroat.

Gale had been fly-fishing long before cutthroats had been so named. People used to call them the Rocky Mountain Spotted trout. Now they were classified into about ten different sub-species that existed in different drainages from New Mexico to Montana. The trout's true birthplace was in Yellowstone Lake in Yellowstone National Park.

The little nine-inch cutthroat almost seemed to be smiling up at him when Gale bent down and palmed it just under the water's surface. Gale smiled back. The immaculate trout mouth was beautiful, simple, small. He kept the fish in the water the whole time, and while holding his rod between his body and his arm, he grabbed the trout's small lower lip with his pointer finger and thumb, and slipped the hook out with his clamps in the other hand. The trout turned back into the living liquid of the river and vanished.

"It is wonderful to catch a fish," Gale thought as he stood in the stream and felt the rushing water run over the rocks and his boots and his fly line and the trout he was trying to catch. The water bound everything together. All the cares the old man had—which were not that many at his age he admitted to himself often— floated downstream with the little cutthroat. They would not return until he left the river. Growing old amid the myriad of ailments that came with that condition, problems with his construction business and its future, problems with his kids who were now raising kids of their own—everything melted into the flowing water, and he was young and dumb and the good kind of wild again.

CHAPTER SEVEN
Big Medicine

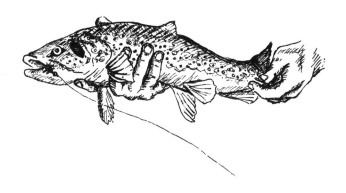

Wilder, as opposed to Gale, was a meat fisherman. Catching a fish meant eating a fish, and the size of his stringer was still the way he judged the success of a trip. There were big trout species in the Rio—rainbow, brook, and brown trout. Wilder intended to catch and keep his limit. Like Gale he carried very little gear, only a flybox, pliers, and the nippers on his neck, but since he expected to eat fish today, a fillet knife dangled from a leather sheath on his belt.

Wilder stood on the riverbank, stripped off 20 feet of line, and made his first cast into the charging water. He watched his pheasant-tail bead head nymph float on top of the water upstream, then he mended his line with his rod tip down, stripping off line as it floated past him and then giving the line back to the fly as it drifted down stream.

He made a roll cast and threw the fly back upstream, then repeated this four or five times to get the fly good and soaked so it would sink to the bottom and act like a nymph swimming under the water's surface. But the water was too fast and it wouldn't sink, so he reeled it back in. He pulled a small selection of split shot from his pocket and took two and placed them 18 inches up from his fly. Then he bit down hard with his molars on the lead weights, securing them to his leader. He cast again, and this time the weight pulled his fly under the water and it disappeared for the length of the drift downstream. Now he was fishing.

Sunny was no fly-fisherman, but she knew her way around a river too. She began to hunt the bank for deep holes and slack water that might hold fish. She didn't take it too seriously, though she hoped to catch a few fish herself. She was unburdened by the inherent fisherman's pride.

So it was with some reluctance that Wilder reeled in and laid down his rod when Sunny hollered at him with an excited "Wilder!" which he knew could only mean one thing—she had a fish on. She was on the bank with her pole sticking straight up in the air and the tip bent almost in half. It was about to break.

"Get your rod tip down! Give him some slack!" Wilder yelled as he ran over to her.

Instead Sunny pressed the button on the

spin cast reel and the rod tip released and line ran out to the fish, which then darted across the river with the freedom it had just been just allowed.

"No, reel that back in, reel and pump him, pump the rod up and down," Wilder instructed, now right next to her.

"OK, OK," Sunny replied, breathless, but with a gravely serious look on her face. She wanted to do well.

The fish had run out of the nice hole it had been in and into the middle of the river, but the heavy 20x test that was on Sunny's line and the heavy hook the worm had been on meant that it was pretty well secured. Sunny began to get the feel for playing it in slowly and did so, pumping the rod up and down between reeling in, feeling the electricity of a heavy fish bouncing and pulling in the water.

"Bring him over to the bank, to that shallow spot, walk downstream a bit," Wilder instructed.

Gale had seen the commotion and laid his rod down too. He wasn't very far away yet. He walked toward the kids.

Sunny played the fish just as Wilder had instructed, and she squealed when she saw the big fish jump in the shallow water and caught the flash of bright silver when his long slick body turned sideways, reflecting the sun for the first time. She brought the fish right to Wilder who was in the water about six inches deep in his Gore-tex hiking boots. Wilder had ordered the boots from the massive Cabela's catalog with birthday money years before. The Gore-tex lining had worn through with his growing feet, and he felt the cold water soak into his socks, which he expected and didn't care about.

Wilder grabbed the large fish with two hands, one hand thumbing the trout's mouth and the other grabbing the tail with a tightly closed fist. As he lifted the fat brown trout, all his ego and jealousy faded. It was just too exciting to pull a large fish from the water.

"What a fish!" he yelled. Sunny laid down her pole and rushed over to him. Wilder handed it to her, and she gripped it with both thumbs in the lower jaw as it dangled and flopped back and forth in the open air. The wild trout was too big to just palm by the belly, especially for her smallish hands. Wilder measured it with the notched inch marks on his rod handle, 24 inches, and it must have been five or six pounds. Wilder thought the fish looked like a massive human bicep flexing and bulging, free of tendons and bones to restrain it. Sunny beamed and giggled as she held the heavy fish away from her thin frame.

"That is some fish, Sunny. Wow, great job," Gale added as he arrived.

The boys stood around Sunny and the dark-speckled fish and admired it, but as Gale and Wilder did they noticed two dime-sized holes on either side of his back, just behind his head. They were deep gaping wounds and you could see the red trout flesh inside of them. Sunny saw them too.

"Gale, what are those?" she asked.

"Well, I have no idea. I have never seen anything quite like that before." He stared at the fish puzzled. "Are you going to keep him? He is legal."

Sunny scrunched up her face, puzzled. In direct contrast to Wilder's approach to fishing, she hadn't really planned on catching any at all. Now she had no idea of whether she wanted to keep it or not.

"Of course she's keeping him," Wilder butted in. "That's a great fish."

"Should I keep him Gale? He looks hurt." Sunny politely ignored Wilder's comment.

"Sunny, hold him down in the water with his head upstream so he can breathe. I want to study him a bit." She did so, stepping both her cowboy boots into the shallow water. Her hands numbed almost immediately in the frigid river.

Gale bent down, grunting on the way, kneeling on the river bank. He felt the sides and back of the submerged fish gently as it began to swivel back and forth and regain his strength. Gale broke into a huge smile.

"I know what this is," the old man chuckled. "From this angle on top it's easy to see. A bald eagle grabbed that fish. Those are talon holes. Or an osprey."

Gale stood up and mused and pinched his lips sideways between his thumb and forefinger. "I have never seen that before. He must have been too big for the bird."

Sunny knew then that she wanted to let it go.

"Wilder, take the hook out please. I want this trout to stay in the river."

Wilder did as she asked and pulled out his needle-nosed fishing pliers from his back pocket. He was disappointed, but he didn't argue. He seemed to understand this fish was kind of special. He grabbed the hook with his pliers and twisted it gently out of the huge trout mouth that had a few spiky teeth and a bottom jaw that hooked up a bit. "What a fish," he thought again.

Sunny cradled the fish in the water after slipping her thumbs out of its mouth, petting it almost. Finally realizing it was free again, the trout gave a mighty swish that broke the water's surface and was gone to the cloudy gray of the river.

The kids rose up, still standing in the water. The trio of fishermen stood there, in a collective exhale of excitement and renewed reverence for their surroundings. They knew they had just seen something beautiful and rare, and it felt kind of overwhelming.

"Wow, that was some fish," Wilder said out loud for the third time, shaking his head back and forth. Sunny smiled, and to Wilder it seemed like she had a tear in one eye.

"That fish," Gale said, "was big medicine. It will be a long time before you see that again."

Big medicine was code language between Wilder and Gale, though it was not intended to keep anything secret from Sunny. Gale always said "big medicine" like some Indian tribes had done in the past, when something remarkable happened in the outdoors. Lewis and Clark had written about it in their journals as they met numerous tribes in the West. It meant something that was more than what it was, like a sign, or something mystical. It was evidence of something spiritual that went past just the physical body of a fish. A fish that had been caught by an eagle and survived.

Whatever big medicine actually meant to either of them, Wilder understood Gale's message and nodded his head in silence. He recognized the importance, and it pleased him.

The wind blew a few wispy blond hairs over Sunny's petite freckled nose, delicate hairs that had escaped her twin braids that had been woven by her mother, Josephine, earlier that morning. She brushed the loose hairs behind her ear and squinted at the sun and its speckled reflection on the river. She bent down and rinsed the fish slime off her hands and was thinking hard about something behind her hazel eyes as she straightened up. She scratched the material just under the collar of her long-sleeved shirt and lifted it up to her nose with her thumb and forefinger. Then she sniffed it. Wilder noticed the strange movement but didn't say anything.

Gale nodded at the kids and smiled and wandered back up the river and found his rod. He moved back and forth working upstream and caught many fish during the morning. One large brown made his reel sing. He never kept any significant drag on his line since he preferred braking the reel with his palm. This let him feel the fish much more acutely. He landed that fish, a fat brook trout about 20 inches and over 5 pounds which is a trophy trout, but Gale returned it too. He hadn't carried a creel in 20 years, although he would eat trout he caught in a lake. On a river, he just wanted to hunt the fish with his rod as if it were a rifle and not be burdened with caring for meat. He loved touching the big and old fish and then letting them swim away, their gnarly hooked jaws pointed upstream in roaring water.

CHAPTER EIGHT
Beard Booger

An hour later it was basically lunchtime, so they gathered back at the truck to eat. Everyone knew the score of the fishing, more or less, though nobody mentioned it—Sunny, one monster fish; Gale, five or six; Wilder, zero. If Sunny hadn't been there Gale would have been calling out all of Wilder's bragging and making him wear it, but Gale knew boys, and girls, so he let his young apprentice have a pass. But now Wilder didn't have any lunch. He just had a rucksack.

Luckily for Wilder, Gale's wife Cille had predictably packed him a sandwich and an apple, and Gale produced them from his folded brown paper grocery sack. Wilder took them and said thank you. He sniffed his hands before handling the sandwich but not to check that they were clean. He was hoping to smell fish on them, knowing that he wouldn't. He had touched Sunny's fish briefly but knew that didn't count.

Sunny was too polite to mention that they weren't eating fish.

They sat on green and fluffy mountain-muhly grass in the shade of the pickup. Gale leaned back against a rear tire. Before Sunny ate her pimiento-cheese sandwich, she presented the group with a stack of cookies she had baked the night before. She took them carefully out of a plastic container and stacked them in a particular pyramid shape on a paper towel, fussing with the presentation before the boys could touch them. The little cookie mound sat on the grass between them. Sunny looked very pleased.

The wildflowers were blooming all around in the canyon, and Gale pointed them out and identified them as they ate: purple lupines with their bonnet-like blooms and seven-fingered green leaves, white mule's ears with rich yellow centers, yellow balsam root with long arrow-shaped leaves, and the glowing red Indian paintbrush that dotted the canyon floor. The Colorado columbines hadn't made their appearance yet, but Gale showed them the plants that would produce the delicate purple and white blooms in July.

When the meal was done and Gale and Wilder had eaten three cookies apiece (and Huck had stolen two), Gale grabbed Wilder's rucksack and folded it up and lay down, using it for a pillow. He stretched out parallel to the pickup and scooted just a bit underneath and knew the shade would not leave him, as the sun was directly overhead now. He had taken his waders off and lay there in his socks. With his eyes closed he told the kids to stay close and stay together.

Wilder and Sunny were tired too, and the admonition to stay close proved unnecessary. They both found sleeping spots, Sunny stretched out in the cab of the pickup and Wilder "bivouacked" in the stand of quaking aspens next to the parking area. He laid his head on Huck's belly, and they both went to sleep quickly, which was unusual for Wilder but not unusual for Huck. Gale snored an old man's deep sleep with a toothpick off to one side of his mouth, as the river and the wind rushed by. The aspens fluttered back and forth like a thousand butterfly wings as they slept.

After they awoke and were stumbling around getting their fishing gear ready for the afternoon, Gale had decided to offer Wilder a bit of advice. Thus far Wilder had been too stubborn to ask what Gale had been catching all his fish on, and there was no way he was going to rig a worm to his fly line like Sunny. But before Gale could speak, a contrite-looking Wilder asked, "What are you fishing with, Gale?"

"Dark flies, big ones. Look like stoneflies and large nymphs. The trout need to see them show up real good in this chocolate milk. They can't see much in the heavy spring runoff."

"Which one exactly?" Wilder asked, but then continued, "I'd like to try it. My pheasant tails aren't working," which was only partly true. Gale's ability to present the flies, and present them in the right part of the river, was probably more important than his fly selection. Gale knew this and knew Wilder would learn, after another thousand hours on the river.

"Beard boogers."

"Beard boogers?" Sunny cracked up. "What is that? It sounds disgusting."

Gale opened his fly box, and the kids came over close. He pinched one from his collection and offered it to Sunny. She scrunched up her nose and moved back. She didn't want to touch it.

Wilder took the large greyish black fly, a size #4, and looked up at Gale.

"It's really called a woolly booger, my favorite fly," Gale explained. "It doesn't look like anything really. It just looks like how a bug should look. I always tied it with grizzly fur from my rug, but I've used so much of it over the years the rug is looking a little sparse. So I told Cille I was going to go to Alaska and kill another one, and she said, 'Yeah right.' She said 'Use your beard, you're woolly booger enough.'

"So I started doing that, and I also renamed them. I call them beard boogers."

Wilder laughed and said "beard booger" out loud.

The old man's eyes sparkled. "Trout seem to like the way I taste."

CHAPTER NINE

Cub Creek

Wilder and Sunny asked permission to work downstream where the river leveled out and the water was smoother and the river wider. Gale let them go and knew there would be more exploring than fishing in the afternoon. Gale trusted Wilder in the outdoors and had carefully taught and observed him on his own, but he always wanted to know where he was and what he was doing. Gale watched over Wilder like a father, even though they weren't related. But he knew he was *fathering* the boy in a real way. Wilder needed the interaction—his dad being so distracted with work and with Livy's care. Livy had been battling breast cancer for several years.

Gale watched the boy on the river and remembered that someone else had done this for him—taken him fishing, watched over him, corrected him, taught him, shown him what it was to be a man. His dad had died when he was five, and an older man had stepped in and helped to raise Gale. That was why Gale loved Wilder all these years later. He was just returning the favor.

Gale didn't insist that they stay within sight-distance, but they agreed to meet back at the truck when the sun first went behind the canyon. Wilder had grabbed his rucksack, another sign that they intended to roam more than fish. Huck had bounded after them.

Wilder was excited to try the beard booger and to get some fish smell on his hands. A boyish sense of competition still lingered over most of what he did. It was something he would grow out of.

Sunny had caught her fill with the one fish and didn't see any reason to keep toting the pole around when she really just wanted to explore. As they walked the footpath along the river, Wilder reached out and grabbed a heart-shaped cottonwood leaf off a large tree that hung over the river. He tore the stem off close to the leaf and took off his hat. He took a dried and withered leaf out of his hat and threw it into the river. He placed the fresh green leaf under the sweatband inside his hat at the front. The "heart" point of the leaf peeked up just over the sweatband about an inch. Then he scrunched the hat back on, the leaf pressed against his forehead. Sunny watched.

"What was that for?"

"Cottonwood leaves keep you cool. Everybody knows that."

Sunny crinkled up her nose. "That's ridonkulous." Sunny liked making up variations on common words. "Ridonkulous" was one of her favorites, and it annoyed Wilder.

"No it's not. My Papa taught me that," Wilder said referring to his Papa Milam who lived in Texas.

"Yep, it's ridonkulous," Sunny repeated.

"Well, maybe I like being ridiculous."

Wilder laughed now and felt at ease with Sunny. Perhaps for the first time in his life, he was becoming comfortable around a girl who wasn't his mother or sister. They walked along the river, both of them about the same size now, although Wilder outweighed the beanpole girl by about 20 pounds. She was thin, but it seemed to Wilder as they walked, that she had recently grown hips.

The two of them trotted along until they came to water that looked right, as Wilder had been taught to read it. It swirled in little surface circles, but the current never broke the surface causing any white water. It was warm now, over 70 degrees, and Wilder noticed little hatches appearing over the surface of the water. Wilder had done very little dry-fly fishing, but he knew that surface bugs were good for underwater action too. It was too early for the trout to feed on the top of the water, but they might be resting in the deep slack water during the hot part of the day.

From the bank he stripped off line and dangled the beard booger and leader about ten feet out into the water. He made two big casts and shot the line out into the smooth water upstream. The tip of his line sank and began slowly bouncing its way down the middle of the river. He mended his line properly as it moved parallel to him. Then his line jerked tight and Wilder felt the electric tug that plugs a fisherman into a trout's underwater world. A fish was on.

He pulled up to set the hook and his rod bent and he let out a "Yahoooo!" that echoed down the canyon and up to Gale who saw his young apprentice with a bent rod. Wilder worked the fish about three times, giving line and letting it run and then reeling the line back in. There was no shallow beach to land it, so Wilder knew he had to tire it out and would have to get it close and grab it from the bank, which he eventually did and soon had an 18-inch "keeper" rainbow in his hands. The silver and red and faint blue fish glimmered in his hands.

Wilder showed Sunny how to gut the fish,

which she knew how to do anyway, but didn't mention it. She liked the way that he wanted to teach her things, even if she already knew many of them. He used the Finland-made fillet knife that dangled from his belt with its long skinny and flexing blade. He threw the guts a few feet up the bank to leave for the coons. Then he searched for a willow sapling with a wide fork and cut it down to make a homemade stringer for all the fish he would catch, which was silly since his limit was only two, and Sunny was now done fishing. He cut a four-foot branch that had a large fork spread at the top. Wilder knew it was early still and they could be on the river another three or four hours and the fish would need to be kept cold. A long stringer branch would allow the fish to be kept in the water while the end of the branch could be secured on the bank. Gale had taught him that.

For the next three hours Wilder and Sunny fished and played and Wilder's fish count filled up on the beard booger's luck. Wilder caught many fish, but most were too small and he was diligent about measuring with them by the inch marks Gale had put on his rod years ago. He had his limit before long, one brown and one rainbow. Sunny had taken charge of the willow stringer and moved it along from place to place as Wilder worked downstream and fished.

At one point they crossed the river, jumping over rocks and downed timber. A bit further on they came upon a 20-foot wide stream that emptied into the Rio from the north. It was running fast and high. There was a forest service sign that read Cub Creek, but there was no improved trail, no footpath, only game trails here and there. It flowed from a different canyon drainage that joined the Rio, which undoubtedly caught a lot of snowmelt. But unlike the cloudy Rio, Cub Creek was flowing clear. Wilder stopped and bent down to take a drink of the fresh bubbling water. To his surprise, in the shallow pool from which he drank, he saw trout in pairs sitting side by side in little dished-shaped gravel beds.

Sunny frowned at Wilder's streamside drinking, but before she could lecture him about the parasite Giardia that swam these rivers, Wilder exclaimed, "Sunny, look at that!" He pointed at the fish, "They're spawning."

Sunny came over and looked in awe at the big fish so close. They were cutthroats, which have bright red streaks at their throats and sometimes belly, especially when spawning. They were swimming in less than a foot of water, and their top fins broke the water's surface. She bent down and tried to grab one. She felt the slippery side of the large trout as it darted upstream, only to return a few seconds after Sunny backed away. Wilder and Sunny were drawn to the wonder and excitement of the rare sighting.

They went from fish to fish, which were paired up every few yards, now working upstream along Cub Creek, which gurgled and splashed but led upwards into the mountains, as opposed to the Rio that was flowing down the wide open canyon. Huck bounced along with them always circling and hunting and sniffing. The woods were dark with tall trees blocking the light, and moss grew on everything in the little creek's floodplain. Going up the stream meant hopping from boulder to boulder, back and forth, shore to shore. Every river and stream and creek has its own personality it seemed to Wilder. They each flowed and fished differently somehow, and Cub creek was dark, like a tunnel going into a rock wall.

There is a trance that mountains and big water can cast, and Wilder and Sunny were now in its grasp. The constant creation of endless and flowing water and changing landscape, and a certain intoxication that beauty can sometimes effect, led them higher and further up the creek.

CHAPTER TEN
Spawning

Gale was sitting on the truck's tailgate early. He figured he had about 20 minutes until the sun hit the high walls of the canyon and the white peaks of the San Juan mountains behind them. He didn't see Wilder and Sunny downriver. From his position he could see about a half-mile of river pretty well. He shook his head, and even though he was tired he grabbed his rod and thought he could at least try some dry fly action while he searched for the kids. He wasn't surprised they were late: he knew they were roaming just like he had done all his life.

Gale walked along the river footpath, which was barely visible with the spring growth and the lack of fishing pressure the river received at this access point. He saw kids' tracks in the mud here and there and saw Wilder's pile of fish guts on the bank. Eventually Gale saw the wet marks on the old pine log where the kids had crossed the river, and while reluctant, he decided to follow. He still had plenty of sun if he found them quickly, but knew he would probably be crossing that log again in the dark. It was two days before a full moon and there would be light, he thought. On the opposite bank he continued to track the kids and had forgotten about fishing and the rod he carried. He wasn't worried yet, but he was now intent only on finding the kids.

About a mile from the truck, he came to where Cub Creek joined the Rio. He stopped and stared at it awhile and saw the spawning cutthroats and went in close to observe them. Like the kids, he was absorbed with the beautiful fish in such a close and vulnerable state. He resisted the childish urge to catch a few with his rod, knowing that breeding fish were easy prey. He didn't figure there was much glory in exploiting an unfair advantage. Besides, the breeding fish meant healthy trout populations for years to come.

He saw kid tracks again, wet rocks and mud and smudged moss on the stream bank and boulders, and he knew they had followed the fish into the woods and up the gently sloping mountain creek. The sun was gone from the canyon now, and the long period of mountain dusk had set in.

The walking was harder along Cub Creek,

slightly uphill and there was no trail, only the winding, splashing mountain creek. Still, he found his way. Gale was strong at 72 and had always liked to be doing. Personally, he feared nothing. Not in a boy's way of being unaware of danger and naïve about injury and death, but he knew what he could and what he could not do, and he had a residing peace about the next life. He was one of the few people who were sure of it.

When he finally came upon Wilder and Sunny they were taking turns sticking their heads under the frigid water, trying to see the fish. He was perplexed at first, and then relieved. There was a large truck-sized pool behind a small waterfall, and from a rock ledge at the surface of the pool Wilder and Sunny were on their hands and knees leaning over the water's surface. They were plunging their heads underwater for as long as they could stand it and watching the fish that must have been spawning in the dark and deep water. Their laughter was barely audible over the crash of the waterfall. Huck sat with them, next to Wilder, clearly having been put into a "sit" and "stay" position to keep him from jumping into the deep pool.

Gale whistled at them from 50 feet away so he wouldn't scare them. Wilder looked up and immediately went a little white as the time and their playfulness hit him. He nudged Sunny and then stood up straight, looking ashamed.

Gale worked his way toward them over the rocks and the narrow bank. Wilder spoke first.

"Gale, I'm sorry. It's my fault. I know it's late."

"Well, yes it is. I need to be able to trust you with time up here. But more important, I need to know where you are."

Sunny nodded and said, "Yes, sir," which made Wilder feel bad again. He knew better and now he knew Sunny felt bad too, even though he had wanted to take the blame.

But Gale never let difficult situations linger too long, and soon they were discussing the spawning cutthroats. He explained the miracle to the kids—the role of the female building the nest, which is called a "redd," and dumping her eggs, and the male joining her and fogging the eggs to fertilize them. And that somehow, years from now, those same tiny trout that were born here, would return to repeat the process, just like their parents were doing now.

"How do they know where to go?" Wilder asked.

"I don't think anybody really can say. But I have always thought it was wise to return home to look for a wife." Gale smiled, amused, if only to himself. He knew the kids wouldn't understand that for a long time. Their faces were blank at his little joke.

"Well, let's go," Gale finally said.

Sunny was eager to please and didn't have to be told twice. She hopped to the lead and hollered over her shoulder, "I'll get the stringer!"

They ascended the steep bank that dropped into the pool with Gale making his huffing and puffing sound as they climbed the 8 feet straight up to the edge of the creek. As soon as they crested the little ridge Sunny stopped and looked at something moving on the stream bank 20 feet ahead, where she had last picketed the stringer of trout.

There were two black bear cubs. And they were eating Wilder's fish, which they had dragged up on the bank.

Sunny paused, but her next instinct was to go towards them. They were fascinating and cute. Without thinking further, she took a step forward, but felt a strong hand on her shoulder. It gripped her and pulled her back with surprising force. She gave into it, and Wilder pulled her back and stepped in front of her.

"The sow is right behind them," he whispered into her ear as he placed himself between her and the three bears.

Wilder slipped a shoulder strap and swung his rucksack off his back and prepared to block the bear with it if she charged, keeping the strong pack between himself and her jaws. His heart was pumping. The sow was big and moving slowly toward them. He had been around bears some, but never this close, and in the near darkness he felt fear rising in him.

The bears had been surprised, just as the people had been. Being surprised, feeding, and with cubs, the old sow was nervous and she woofed at the people ahead of her in the dim light. It was a powerful deep "WOOF" that came from a muzzle lined with jagged white teeth.

Gale heard the "woof" and knew exactly what it was. He was atop the steep, narrow trail now, standing behind the two kids. He knew making a move toward the bears was dumb and might provoke an attack, but he couldn't let Wilder take a possible charge head-on. He touched Sunny from behind and maneuvered her behind him on the trail. Then he grabbed for Wilder, who submitted, although braced with his pack and gritted teeth. Gale stood square in front of the two kids and cleared his throat.

The sow stood up on her back legs like a person and seemed to squint at them. She tilted her head high to wind the strange animals in her path. Undecided on their identity, she barked at her cubs in bear language. They immediately retreated uphill and began scrambling up a large pine tree.

The big bear was now eye to eye with the old man. She stood on the trail motionless, six feet tall. Gale was six-feet-one, and it seemed to him as if a massive furry man was in front of him. The cubs climbed the tree to his right making no sounds except for tiny bear claws gripping bark. The momma bear looked right into Gale's eyes and dropped back to all fours. Then she began moving toward him swinging her head side to side slowly and snapping her jaws. It sounded like *pop*, *pop*, *pop*, backed up by a low rumbling growl. Her ears were fully erect and facing forward. There was nothing for Gale to do but stand his ground.

At ten feet the bear charged.

CHAPTER ELEVEN

Mother Bear

Gale had pulled his lock-blade pocket knife from his front pocket that was hidden beneath his waders. He opened it and held it ready in his right hand, having thrown down his rod. He knew most bear charges were only bluffs, as he had been charged by a few bears in the past, but the conditions of this encounter were all set against him. He didn't want to fight or hurt the bear, but he knew that in a real attack, fighting back was the best way to survive. But if a full grown 350-pound black bear wanted to kill a person, he knew there was little he could do.

But if she was going to bluff him, Gale was going to bluff her right back. And if she hit him he could at least bring the knife down and bury the four inch blade deep into her neck.

The bear covered the ten feet in two big bear lopes; and in the same instant in which she covered that distance, the old man raised his hands high above his head as if he were also a bear, made claws with his fingers, drew in all the mountain air he could hold, and roared at the top of his lungs.

"RAAAAAAAAR!"

The mighty sound shocked Wilder and Sunny, as it did the bear. Gale's roar echoed down the canyon drainage. Whether she had been planning a bluff charge or not, she braked herself and slid right into Gale's feet with force, causing him to stumble back. She was turning around as she slid to a stop.

As Gale stepped back to get his balance, Huck, who had been scrambling up the bank behind the trio, flew past them on the trail barking for all his worth. He ran past the kids and launched himself from behind Gale into the turning bear.

Huck, all 80 pounds and tail like a crowbar, knocked the unbalanced Gale off the trail and back down into the creek. The old man took the eight-foot fall in silence as Wilder and Sunny watched in panic. He landed in the deep water and submerged rocks at the end of the large pool. His legs fell into shallower water near the bank, while his body fell into the black depth of the pool. As the current grabbed him, his whole body went completely under for a few seconds. Several yards downstream at the base of the pool, Gale's head and arms popped up to the surface again. He was trying to swim.

Wilder stood there in shock as Huck and the black bear did somersaults ripping and growling and flipping each other in a primal contest for life. He couldn't tell what was happening or who was getting hurt. The sudden ferocious violence of the animals froze him. The black and tan ball of fur and claws and teeth turned over and over on the path in front of him. Then he heard Gale holler his name.

Wilder turned slowly from his stupor to see Gale bouncing up and down in the fast current of the pool. He could not regain his footing or make any headway in swimming to the steep bank. It seemed like he should have just been able to walk out and Wilder couldn't understand why he didn't.

Wilder scrambled down the bank, with Sunny right behind him. He reached for Gale and grabbed one of his arms. He couldn't pull him up, or out. It was as if Gale was anchored to the bottom in the fast cold water.

Gale was out of breath from swimming with his arms, but he managed to mutter to Wilder, "Cut off my waders . . ."

Wilder's eyes went wide, and he realized that his old man was drowning. Sunny felt the fear too, and let out a small scream. She was reaching for Gale, but there was no room for her to grab hold of his other arm.

Wilder knew he couldn't let go of the hand he had. He would not. He feared if he let go Gale would be sucked to the bottom just like the elk earlier that morning. But he knew he had to act. Wilder had been told a thousand times by his dad and Gale, "Figure it out," and although he didn't remember the exact words at the time, the nature of the training came back to him now. He knew he must figure it out. The first problem was that he had to get closer to Gale to cut the wader straps that were over his shoulders. It was the straps that were pulling him under the icy water.

Above them in the forest the furious dog and bear fight had gone silent.

Wilder jerked his fillet knife out of its sheath at his belt and placed the wooden handle into his mouth sideways—like the pirates in *Treasure Island*, which he had watched so many times. Still holding onto Gale's hand he dropped into the deep cold water. It took his breath away and scared him. But gathering himself mentally, he let the current push him up to Gale's backside. This propped Gale up some as both Wilder's swimming legs and the strong current provided support to Gale's backside. He slid his left hand off of Gale's arm and hugged him tightly with that whole arm now, firm around Gale's chest. With his other free hand, Wilder grabbed the knife out of his mouth.

Working in unspoken unison, Sunny had taken Wilder's place on the bank and now held Gale's arm securely, her two hands tight around it. Her fingers didn't touch around the thick forearm, but with both hands she had a white-knuckled grip.

Wilder knew he had to work quickly, and he hoped the knife would do its job on the tough Kevlar straps. He poked the skinny blade under the first strap and felt Gale tighten as the blade tip must have stabbed into the top of his shoulder. Wilder couldn't hold the strap up to cut it, so he just had to work the blade under the strap as best he could, a strap that was mashed deeply into Gale's shoulder by the hundreds of pounds of water pressure.

He knew that he cut the old man some as he wiggled the blade sideways and up and sawed through Gale's wool shirt and the two-inch-wide strap. Eventually the strap began to fray, so he kept nudging the knife forward, knowing he was cutting into Gale's shoulder.

Finally the strap broke free, and Gale popped up several inches with half of the waders now released. Wilder now hoped Gale could just wiggle out of the second strap. He tossed the knife onto the shore next to Sunny. And he felt himself beginning to numb from the cold water.

"Gale, wiggle your shoulder out of the other strap, and we will have you."

Gale heard him and did so, and when the second strap slipped off his shoulder, he floated up and free, level with Wilder. The waders disappeared below the water in an instant as if sucked down by a giant vacuum.

Wilder clung to Gale's back as Sunny pulled them over to the bank, with a hand now on each of Gale's hands. He couldn't grip her back with much force, and it scared her to feel his strength sagging.

Sunny buoyed him, and Wilder let go and climbed up the bank, shooting himself up and catching a knee on the ledge. Gale tried to do the same as Sunny pulled up with all her strength, but when he did he let out a wincing "Owww." Wilder had never heard a sound like that from him before.

On the bank now, Wilder grabbed onto one of Gale's arms and the two kids held on to the old man, looking down at him in the water as they leaned over on their knees.

"Wilder," Gale said panting, "I'm pretty sure my leg is broke. You're going to have to pull me out of here. Each one you get on one arm and pull me downstream over the rocks to where it gets shallow. Do it now. Do not stop."

Wilder nodded, scared, but thriving on the urgency of the moment. He recovered and sheathed his knife with one hand and tightened his grip on Gale's arm. He and Sunny stood up in unison, raising Gale slightly higher out of the water. Wilder looked at Sunny and nodded at her with steel in his eye and was a bit surprised to see the same look reflected back at him. He saw her set her jaw tight and noticed a tiny snarl rise up in her upper lip and nostril. She was ready.

They pulled as hard as they could and flinched in sympathetic pain as Gale came out of the water and his legs banged on the rocks. They worked him with the current, downstream just like a fish. They didn't know which leg was broken, but they noticed how limp his legs were as his body moved across the rocks and onto the shore at last.

The old man never made a sound.

〜ᏻ™

CHAPTER TWELVE

'Not to worry'

Wilder and Sunny moved Gale away from the water's edge. As soon as they stopped dragging him Sunny moved to cradle his head in her hands and lap. The sun was down now and the nearly full moon hadn't crested the canyon sky yet. Gale looked up at Sunny and smiled at the young girl. He was numb with cold and exhaustion and pain from his leg, but he felt the warmth of a female's care. Her face was like a light and he felt at peace.

"What do you want me to do, Gale? Go for help?" Wilder panted, dripping with frigid water. He was on his knees, leaning over Gale, his eyes searching his mentor for instruction.

Gale was limp in his body, and it took him awhile to answer. Old age hadn't sapped his strength, but what it had stolen first was his endurance. The creek had taken all his energy. He felt like a gutted fish lying there wet and cold and partly broken.

"Not to worry," he said with conviction, if

weakly and of habit. "Let's just make this little trip a campout too."

"What do you mean campout?" Wilder was incredulous. "We have to get you out of here."

"Wilder, listen to me. We'll be just fine." Gale closed his eyes. "Get a fire going if you can.

"Not to worry," the old man repeated a second later.

Wilder sensed a crushing reality that Gale was not completely himself. He had never felt the weight of decision-making in such circumstances before. He felt alone and panicky.

Wilder stood up and looked around. Huck was missing, a sow black bear was in the woods, her two cubs were probably still up a tree within 50 feet of them. Gale had a broken leg and was perhaps close to hypothermia, and they were in wilderness in the dark several miles from the pickup.

And nobody knew where they were.

The young boy's mind raced. He bounced back and forth between fear and reluctance, to a stubborn demand for action. He couldn't think straight in either direction.

Wilder bent down and whispered in Sunny's ear, "I have to hike out of here. Get help."

As Sunny turned her head to her friend, her face wore a tranquility he didn't expect.

"No you don't," she whispered. "That would

only make it worse. Do what Gale said. "Make a fire. My . . ."

"But . . ." he interrupted.

"No," she raised her voice slightly, cutting him off. The steel that had been in her eye was now in her voice, "My dad is coming. He will be here soon. I know it."

Wilder stopped his belligerent reply. He knew she was right. He stood back up. His quick action had saved Gale in the water, but now was the time to slow down. They needed to stay put and take care of Gale together.

Sunny had begun to unbutton Gale's wool shirt. He seemed to be sleeping, but was shivering.

Wilder knew what he needed to do now. He scrambled up the bank and located his rucksack. His first-aid kit and assorted other items were in there, including his matches. He grabbed the space blanket—the one he had packed on a hundred previous outings because a survival book had told him to do so, even though he figured he would never use it. He brought it to a now shirtless Gale and wrapped it around his pasty white torso.

Sunny whispered to Wilder to cut off Gale's jeans. He pulled his fillet knife out again. After removing Gale's socks he carefully sliced up both legs to Gale's mid-thigh and then cut the cold cotton jeans away. Sunny spread the shiny and crinkly blanket over his body. Wilder returned to his rucksack and found his waterproof match container.

There was deadfall everywhere in the forest, but Gale was still lying in the damp floodplain of the creek. They would have to move him again even if just a few feet. Wilder selected the nearest dry place, about ten feet away and a few feet higher in elevation. Like most boys who are fascinated with fire, Wilder was a master at starting campfires. And he believed a true outdoorsman should start a fire with only one match. Which he did and within a few minutes he had a nice blaze going that lit the entire creek bed and flashed up and down on the giant evergreens that surrounded them like ancient stone pillars.

He returned to Sunny, and they discussed moving Gale the ten feet to the fire. They gave his shoulders a slight preliminary tug, but the old man grunted in pain. Beneath closed eyes he spoke, "Wilder, splint my leg first. The left one, below the knee." That was all he said and then seemed to drift off again.

Wilder shrugged and returned quickly to the forest. He had never splinted a broken leg before, but as he had read numerous survival guides, he remembered the basic procedure:

Try not to move a broken leg because the fractured bones can stab into the flesh and blood vessels of the leg and cause internal bleeding, not to mention excruciating pain. He had to immobilize the leg to give it superficial skeletal support. Wilder rummaged in the downed timber and broke two, two-foot-long pieces of pine, each about four inches in diameter.

Bringing them back to Gale, he retrieved the large roll of medical webbing from his first aid kit. Next to Gale's exposed left leg he put the two splint sticks and began wrapping them softly, but he didn't like the way the webbing seemed to press the rigid sticks into Gale's leg. He stopped and unwound the first loop. He took Gale's wet woolen shirt and wrung it out and removed the old man's gold handled fishing clamps that hung on the pocket. He clamped them on his own shirt flap so they wouldn't get lost, but he liked having done it and immediately felt stronger, older, wearing them on his chest like a badge. Knowing the wool shirt would still insulate even if wet, he cradled Gale's leg in it, wrapping the leg twice, and then proceeded to apply the wraps around the entire splint.

Satisfied with the job after a careful two minutes, he was eager for his Gale to feel the warmth of the fire. Sunny stood up and stumbled a bit in the dark. One leg had gone to sleep under Gale's weight. She steadied herself as best she could, and the pair looped their arms under the old man's shoulders and started their drag. Gale was silent as his leg bounced over the ground and each exposed stone. At least the leg was in a good splint this time, Wilder thought, pleased with his work.

When they got near the fire Sunny once again held Gale's head while Wilder placed his empty rucksack under her. Once again she sat down, cradling the old man's head as before.

Wilder returned to the creek with his Nalgene water bottle and submerged it as he bent down and slurped a big drink himself. Back at the fire Wilder handed the water bottle to Sunny, who offered it to Gale's lips first. He took a slow drink that made the kids feel relieved. Sunny drank too and then handed the bottle back to Wilder. He tightened the lid and set it down next to her.

The campfire light leapt and shone dramatically in the reflective space blanket that encased Gale. It was a striking and encouraging light. Gale looked like he was wrapped in a large liquid-orange cocoon. At last Wilder sat down—for the first time, perhaps, since lunch—and felt the shock of what had just happened. His mind raced through the bear and

Huck and the creek and the fire and moving Gale. It all seemed a blur that just kept repeating itself over and over, like watching the wooden horses go up and down and round and round on a carousel. His stomach felt sick.

Wilder was cold and drenched to the bone. He realized he was shivering too, so he stood up and hovered over the fire. If Sunny hadn't been there he would have stripped off some clothes, but the night was still relatively warm and the fire made his hair and clothes dry fast.

"Wilder, why don't you catch us some fish?" Sunny said encouragingly from across the fire when it seemed like his body temperature had returned to normal.

Wilder looked up from the flames, surprised at the thought, but relieved that his mind had something to chew on. He nodded to Sunny and wandered out of the light, upstream to the waterfall at the top of the big pool that he had just jumped into rescuing Gale. He found his rod, and as he stooped to pick it up, something huge splashed into the pool.

Wilder had been too distracted to be scared of anything in the dark just yet, but the large explosion of water startled him to his core. He froze and gripped his rod tight, prepared to use it as a weapon if needed.

But he soon recognized the breathing and

smooth, even sound of a swimming dog . . . his dog. In the waning moonlight he saw the long lab nose and floppy ears of Huck churning his way. He was relieved and with excitement called out, "Huck!" The dog came to Wilder and leaped up on the stone perch he had sat on with the kids only 15 minutes before. The happy dog shook himself in a little canine earthquake that sprayed and soaked Wilder again. Wilder felt him up and down for injuries and fingered numerous squishy gashes in his coat. There was a two-inch rip in his right ear. It made a little flap that hung down like a wet paper towel. Despite those battle wounds the dog was sound and overall unharmed. He panted contentedly next to his master.

Wilder carried his rod back to the campfire so he could tie on a new set-up with a little light. He and Huck bounded into the firelight with fresh hope. Sunny cried out saying, "HUCK!!!" and gave him the warmest dog hug possible as he presented himself nose to nose and licked the girl's face once as if to say, "Aw, I'm fine. Happy to have saved the day." He wagged his tail furiously and wandered all over the campfire's glowing circle of light, seemingly unaware of the risk and fear the kids had faced, much of it his fault . . . due to a dog's twin gifts of bravery and belligerence.

Wilder sat and nipped off the beard booger from his tippet and carefully seated it in the Hall of Fame on his hat. As he did so, he had to smile. Then he rigged a hopper-dropper from the flies in his fly case. He took a large grass-hopper fly, a #4, and tied it to his tippet. Then he tied the pheasant-tail bead head he had used that morning to the hook on the hopper, with about 24 inches of tippet between them. The hopper was a dry fly that would work as a sur-face bobber, capable of catching fish itself and also keeping the bead head at about the middle of the water's depth.

He went back to the deep waterfall pool and cast the two-fly rig into the middle. He laid his rod down and placed a big rock on top of the reel. He set the drag as tightly as he could and hated to leave a light fly rod in such a rough position, but he knew it was his only hope to catch any more fish and not lose his rod to the bottom of the pool.

Back at the fire Wilder checked that Gale's splint wasn't too tight, fed a few dried sticks to the fire, and then plopped down, leaning back on a deadfall log. Wilder and Sunny didn't know it, but as they sat scared and alone in the woods, two tiny black bear cubs peered down on them.

CHAPTER THIRTEEN
Two Cubs

Around midnight the cubs started crying to their mother. They sounded like human babies sniffling and moaning in a crib. It was strange, and frightened the kids at first until Huck jumped up and barked at them. He found their tree, a large Ponderosa pine, which wasn't 20 feet off from the campfire, and sent up some hound-like howls to the upper branches. Wilder and Sunny figured the mother wasn't far off either, but she was keeping her distance from the strong people smell and the fire and from Huck. Throughout the night Huck would wake from sleep, his hackle would rise on his shoulders and down his back, and he would growl to a bear he could only sense in the darkness. Wilder never saw anything, but he knew to trust his dog. Huck would sound the alarm, although he was too tired and perhaps fearful now, to charge off into the black woods again. Each time the dog awoke, he walked over to Gale and licked his hand.

Wilder caught several smallish trout and

even retrieved the large Brown on the willow stringer that the bears had partially eaten. He cut fresh willow saplings from the creek bottom and made a criss-cross grill of sorts for roasting the pink flesh, splayed open down the middle. The green willows didn't burn, and the trout needed only minutes to cook on the hot pine fire. The skin and bones peeled off the cooked trout meat easily. Wilder let Sunny eat first. She shook Gale gently and tried to offer him some, but he didn't respond so she let him sleep. Huck ate the fish guts and bones and skin like a wolf, slurping and crunching them in the darkness. He was a country dog and as such hadn't been introduced to canned dog food. He ate what he could get.

Wilder looked across the fire and studied Sunny. He thought that propping up Gale's head was a bit much at this point. Wilder wouldn't have held Gale's head all night. He was fine, it seemed; warm and dry and safe. Wilder was pleased and felt like he had done everything that was needed. He wasn't happy about all the danger the night had brought them and the fact that they were still lost up a mountain creek, but it was also true, in a way, that he was enjoying every moment. He was being tested in the wilderness and it felt wonderful to be surviving. He would have started building a log cabin with his fillet knife that night, if only someone had suggested it.

Sunny sat on Wilder's rucksack and leaned back on a log like Wilder. She occasionally caressed Gale's forehead. The fire flickered and flashed on the thick pines they sat under. Wilder felt the warm and sickening feeling return to him as he looked at her, the feeling that he had lost sometime during the day as she had become just another friend on the river. The feeling that he had no word for yet, but that he was old enough now to suppose it was . . . love. He felt a magnetic pull towards her, and yet it was pure and innocent, for it held no desire. It was a mystery to him.

"Wilder, what is your favorite thing?" Sunny asked in the yellow and orange glow of the campfire. It seemed obvious now that they were in for a long night and neither seemed to be giving in to sleep.

"Ummm . . ." Wilder mumbled, his mind far off from his favorite things.

"I know what mine is," Sunny bubbled up.

"OK, what?" Wilder knew he was supposed to take the bait and ask now.

"Dip cones from Dairy Queen. I wish I had one right now."

"I guess they are good," Wilder agreed.

"I think they are the perfect thing. They're delicious but they're also a challenge. Once you start in on one you have to strategically work your way around. The chocolate crust starts breaking up and moving fast. My mom calls them 'pangeas' because they look like the Earth's crust breaking apart." Sunny giggled at this.

"And you want to have the right combination of chocolate and ice cream with each bite. And that's another thing—you can't just lick, you have to bite *and* lick. In Texas they call them 'brown derbies' 'cause they look like those old fashioned hats. Did you know that?"

"No."

"Well, that's my favorite thing right now. What's yours?"

Wilder couldn't bring it up that fast, but he decided to consider it and give her an answer. The fire crackled between them and he thought about it for a while.

"I guess it is this: Being out in the country with my gear and seeing stuff. Climbing rocks and catching fish and just looking for some new thing to run to down the trail."

"Me too." Sunny paused, "But I like being home too." She turned her head and scratched the place on her shirt just beneath her collar.

She pinched the cloth and brought it to her nose and seemed to sniff deeply at the material.

"Why do you do that?" Wilder had noticed her doing the same thing several times that day.

"My mom's perfume. She sprays it there when I leave the house on a big trip. She wears Chanel Chance. I love the smell, and it fills me up when I start to feel a little empty."

"Ohh," Wilder said, but Sunny's mention of her mom sent his thoughts back to his own mother, and Sunny saw it in the hollow look in his eyes.

"I'm sorry about your mother, Wilder. I pray for her."

Wilder nodded, and did so making eye contact so she could see he received her comment. It was on account of Livy's breast cancer that Wilder spent so much time with Gale. His dad spent most of his time working or caring for Livy.

"How is she?"

"Well, she is up and down I guess. I watch her, and I read books about cancer in the library. Sometimes I want to talk about it a lot, and sometimes I don't."

Sunny nodded, returning his eye contact across the fire.

"I guess *she* is my favorite thing. And I never want it to end."

They sat and watched the fire, and they both felt a little uneasy. They knew they were talking about big things, which they hadn't ever done before. Wilder marveled at himself, how words that he had never put together before could just roll right out of his mouth.

"Why did you punch Boone?" Sunny broke the tension with a question she had been planning to ask at some point.

"I don't know," Wilder answered with the same answer a boy has for everything, especially the dumb stuff they do.

"I guess I was crying and throwing a big fit about it, but you didn't have to punch him," Sunny said, more amused than corrective.

Wilder stared at the fire, and his mind returned to the cafeteria, to the fight.

"I guess I love you, Sunny," Wilder blurted out without really thinking, kind of like the punch. "I always have."

Sunny was surprised with the boldness of the answer, but she smiled. She didn't say anything in reply. Wilder replayed the words in his head and realized what he had said out loud. It was something he had said in his mind many times, and it had just kind of spilled out like hot coffee sloshing out of a cup.

"You won't always be able to go off wildering, you know," Sunny said—joking again, lightening the conversation, sort of. Sunny had far-off feelings for Wilder too.

"What?"

"It's what you do. Wilder goes wildering. All over the place, you're like a bobcat, or a bear. You just wander around being as wild as you can."

"Yeah, well. That's what I like."

"You'll have to get married and have kids and get a job someday."

"Nope. I won't."

"You will."

Wilder was kind of annoyed. He had said too much already, and now he was getting told what to do. He was ready to change the subject.

"You really think your Dad is on his way?" Wilder asked, resuming his naïve and slightly argumentative tone.

"Oh, my dad will come, Wilder. I know that. I am sure he is looking for me right now."

"How do you know?"

"I just know. He won't sleep until he has me. He calls me his 'best.'"

"His 'best' what?"

"I don't know," Sunny pondered, never having thought of it that way. "I guess his best anything . . . and everything." She smiled, satisfied with that answer.

"My dad has my heart right now, Wilder.

But he told me that someday he will give some of it back . . . and that part will be mine to give to someone else." And that was the last they spoke of love and hearts and things like that for a long time.

Then Sunny started humming, and the humming led to singing in the dark woods up Gallinas canyon. It surprised Wilder and kind of surprised Sunny too. She hadn't planned to sing. It was a song she had been writing in her head all day, and now she wanted to hear it. It had begun when she had released the wounded trout. She sang brave and loud, and though she was only one voice, Wilder thought he heard a harmonizing with the echoes of the trees and rocks and water. She sang,

I see my
Jesus on the River,
He's walking,
And watching the flow,
He's here,
But he's there,
I know,
Seeing his loss,
Waiting to cross . . .
my
Jesus on the River.

Wilder smiled and, for the first time, was sure that he loved Sunny Parker. He also knew that someday, he would give up wildering for her. He just wouldn't tell her.

〰

CHAPTER FOURTEEN
Gallinas Canyon

Sunny was right about her dad. Jack Parker had left the house at eleven PM, an hour after the latest he had expected to see Gale Loving's pickup in his driveway. He trusted Gale as much as he trusted himself, but he knew that anything could happen in wild country. Gale had a cell phone, but he had left it in his truck, and so after repeated no-answers, Jack set out to find them. Gale hated having a phone on him, especially on a river, and the cell coverage was spotty at best anyway, so it really didn't matter. Jack had called Wilder's father, Hank, who was on the other side of the state on a construction job in Fort Collins. Hank was on his way now; he had told Jack that he would call Lucille Loving and keep her informed.

Jack drove the hour to the river and checked every access point for Gale's truck. Around three AM he spotted the pickup. He called out for the kids, but the roaring river drowned his voice out quickly. On his cell phone he called the search-and-rescue number. He was a local member, and he knew his buddies would be rousing out of bed and coming to help soon.

He looked at the river sparkling in the moonlight and knew they would have fished upstream the way fly-fishermen do. So he took off with his flashlight in the logical, but wrong direction from where his daughter and Wilder and Gale were camped. He walked a mile down, crossed the river in the darkness, and returned down the other side. He made out some of their tracks but everything seemed to lead back to the truck.

Around four-thirty some of the search-and-rescue team arrived, they synced their radios and spread out with flashlights. Jack walked downriver, and while he was a long way from panic, he felt a tightness in his chest that his daughter could be in danger—a feeling that he knew wouldn't leave until he had a head count. She had always been with him since she was born, working cattle, hunting, fishing, church. He never forced her to go, but she always stayed there, right on his hip. Since her birth he felt that she *was* him in some way, and it startled him. She was the most unexpected thing that had ever happened to him.

When Jack found the footprint mud smears on the log bridge that Wilder and Sunny and

Gale had crossed, his hopes revived. He followed the bridge across and saw Cub Creek a quarter of a mile to the north. He jogged to the confluence of the two waters and studied the ground with his flashlight beam. The early mountain morning was coming on, and a blue-tinged backlight rose behind the mountains to the east.

Jack saw the spawning cutthroats and knew the kids must have seen them too. He crossed Cub Creek and followed the Rio for 100 yards more, but he saw no kids' tracks. So he turned around and started up Cub Creek, boulder to boulder like the kids had done earlier.

Fifteen minutes later he smelled the campfire. When he crested the creek bottom and looked up to see his daughter sitting around a campfire with Gale and Wilder, their eyes locked onto each other, and he knew she was OK. She smiled at him, and those huge bent teeth shot right through him. He gritted his teeth and fought every emotion and nodded at her. Gale was sitting up now, smiling weakly and leaning against the log next to Sunny. His legs were straight out in front of him, which looked unnatural, not to mention that he was wearing what amounted to cut-off jean shorts. His wool shirt was on again, though buttoned unevenly, and his gray hair spiked up all around like a birds nest. He had a toothpick in his mouth. He looked ridiculous. He was fine.

Keeping her seat, Sunny looked over at Wilder, who had been carving on a branch. She nodded at him coolly and said, "See, I told you he would come."

Then the little girl sprang up and ran to her father yelling "Daddy!!!" all the way. Jack hugged her and spun her in the air and called her his "best," burying his nose in her now quite loose braids.

Jack did a quick check of everyone's condition, and Gale rose up on one leg with a green pine crutch that Wilder had rigged for him during the night. Jack insisted that he was going to call for a helicopter, and Gale insisted just as forcefully that he was not. Jack then radioed the search-and-rescue team on the river and told them to bring a rescue board to carry Gale out, which made Gale mad. He said he was fine and that the kids had saved his life. Jack called Hank, who was driving fast down I-25 now, and told him the kids were safe and with him.

The search-and-rescue guys soon arrived and cajoled Gale into being strapped onto the board. Gale hated this, but he didn't really have a choice. They re-splinted the leg and bragged about the job Wilder had done. Wilder just nodded, but his chest was puffing out pretty good. Sunny looked at him with admiration as she clung to her dad's side.

While everybody was tending to Gale, and Wilder was telling the story in a feigned "aw shucks" manner, Sunny accidentally kicked the stick that Wilder had been carving all night. She looked to make sure he wasn't watching and picked up the bright piece of freshly carved pine. He had either forgotten about it or had just simply thrown it away. As she rolled the small stick over in her hands she saw that it read in jagged knife marks, WILDER + SUNNY, and something inside the young girl broke a little. She inhaled just a bit and knew the piece of her heart that her dad had told her about was starting to drift away. She hid the stick up her sleeve.

The two black bear cubs were still in the tree, and everybody got a good look at them. They were clinging to each other high above the ground, peering down at the people with shiny black eyes. As they all walked out of the campground, Sunny yelled back at the cubs, which had unknowingly caused so much trouble, "Goodbye, little guys!"

Wilder and Sunny drove home with Jack Parker as the sun came up in the front windshield, blinding them all a bit. Jack put his sun glasses on and pulled the visor low, casting a shadow into the front seat of the pickup cab. Sunny sat next to her dad with Wilder next to her. Wilder leaned back and over a bit against the door and laid his head back. He closed his eyes but didn't sleep. He held his hat in his hands on his lap.

Huck lay all by himself on the backseat floorboard. He licked his wounds with an annoyingly loud sound and a goofy yet unaware dignity, as only dogs can do.

Sunny launched into an energetic retelling of every piece of the day and night with both hands buzzing up and down and left and right and making big growls for Huck and the bear and repeating Gale's blood-curdling roar. She made a special point of saying how brave Wilder was and how he had saved Gale's life. She left out the part where Wilder wanted to charge off into the night, and how she had probably saved his life by keeping him in one place.

"And Dad, I did like you always tell me. We stayed put. We made good 'little decisions.'"

Jack Parker listened, silent and nodding as he watched the road. When she finished he cleared his throat, causing Wilder to open his eyes and look at him. He looked over at both kids on the seat next to him.

"Well, you two certainly didn't need to be

rescued. You did everything just right. There were no chickens up Gallinas Canyon last night."

He grabbed Sunny with one arm and held her close. He looked back up at the road and chuckled once to himself and then inhaled deep and breathed out very low and long. The exhale let go of all the terrors and visions that only a parent can know. His daughter was safe.

"What do chickens have to do with it, Dad?" Sunny asked with a puzzled face.

"*Gallinas*, that means chickens. In Spanish."

"Oh . . ." Sunny laughed and mused. She looked up at her Dad and said, "It was a great adventure, Dad. And I feel kinda different now.

"The night really wasn't that long."

Wilder smiled but kept quiet. He caught a little smell of fish and looked down at his hands resting on the top of his hat. He raised them to his face and sniffed them both. He smiled again and closed his eyes. This would be a good story to tell Molly.

It took a week for the fish smell to wear off.

THE END

ᴠᴄ

ABOUT THE AUTHOR

S. J. Dahlstrom lives and writes in West Texas with his wife and children. A fifth-generation Texan, S. J. has spent his life "bouncing around" the countryside from New Mexico and Texas, north to Colorado and Montana, and east to Michigan and New York. He is interested in all things outdoors and creative. He writes poetry  and hunts deer; he plants wildflowers and breaks horses; he reads Ernest Hemingway and Emily Dickinson and C. S. Lewis and Søren Kierkegaard.

S. J.'s writing draws on his experiences as a cowboy, husband, father—and as a founder of the Whetstone Boys Ranch in Mountain View, Missouri. He says, "I wrote this story about Wilder Good for kids who grew up in the outdoors and for kids who long for the outdoors . . . working, fishing, hunting; farms, ranches, mountains and prairies. I think all kids want to do these things and go to these places." THE ADVENTURES OF WILDER GOOD is his first book series.

You can learn more about S. J. Dahlstrom and join Wilder Good on his adventures when you visit the Wilder Good website, *www.WilderGood.com*, where S. J. encourages readers to 'Be Wilder' and submit photos and stories about their own adventures.

Coming Soon!

#5

THE ADVENTURES OF
WILDER GOOD

BLACK ROCK
BROTHERS

3 1170 01151 9406

CPSIA information can be obtained
at www.ICGtesting.com
Printed in the USA
LVHW01s1426230218
567702LV00001B/1/P

9 781589 881006